It's Checkup Time!

Publisher Margot Schupf
Vice President, Finance Vandana Patel
Executive Director, Marketing Services Carol Pittard
Executive Director, Business Development Suzanne Albert
Executive Director, Marketing Susan Hettleman
Publishing Director Megan Pearlman
Associate Director of Publicity Courtney Greenhalgh
Assistant General Counsel Simone Procas
Assistant Director, Special Sales Ilene Schreider
Assistant Director, Finance Christine Font
Senior Manager, Sales Marketing Danielle Costa
Senior Manager, Children's Category Marketing Amanda Lipnick
Senior Manager, Business Development + Partnerships Nina Fleishman Reed
Senior Production Manager Susan Chodakiewicz
Marketing Manager Isata Yansaneh
Associate Prepress Manager Alex Voznesenskiy
Assistant Project Manager Hillary Leary

Editorial Director Stephen Koepp
Art Director Gary Stewart
Senior Editors Roe D'Angelo, Alyssa Smith
Managing Editor Matt DeMazza
Editor, Children's Books Jonathan White
Copy Chief Rina Bander
Design Manager Anne-Michelle Gallero
Assistant Managing Editor Gina Scauzillo
Editorial Assistant Courtney Mifsud

Produced by DOWNTOWN BOOKWORKS INC.

President Julie Merberg
Editorial Director Sarah Parvis
Editorial Assistant Sara DiSalvo
Editorial Intern Olivia Galvez
Cover and Interior Design Georgia Rucker

SPECIAL THANKS: Chelsea Alon, Allyson Angle, Curt Baker, Katherine Barnet, Brad Beatson, Jeremy Biloon, John Champlin, Ian Chin, Rose Cirrincione, Assu Etsubneh, Mariana Evans, Alison Foster, Kristina Jutzi, David Kahn, Jean Kennedy, Samantha Long, Amy Mangus, Kimberly Marshall, Robert Martells, Nina Mistry, Melissa Presti, Danielle Prielipp, Babette Ross, Dave Rozzelle, Matthew Ryan, Ricardo Santiago, Divyam Shrivastava, Krista Wong

Published by Time Home Entertainment Inc.
1271 Avenue of the Americas, 6th floor • New York, NY 10020

ISBN 10: 1-61893-377-9
ISBN 13: 978-1-61893-377-5

We welcome your comments and suggestions about Time Home Entertainment books. Please write to us at:

Time Home Entertainment books
Attention: Book Editors
P.O. Box 11016
Des Moines, IA 50336-1016

If you would like to order any of our hardcover Collector's Edition books, please call us at 800-327-6388, Monday through Friday, 7 a.m.–8 p.m., or Saturday, 7 a.m.–6 p.m., Central Time.

1 QGW 15

Welcome to Doc McStuffins' clinic for stuffed animals and toys! Here you'll find extra big doses of friendship, caring, and cuddles. So join Doc and all her toys and have some fun!

Each page of this book is a poster. Cut them out, hang them up, and enjoy! Doc's orders!

DOC AND FRIENDS

Every day is fun
when you spend it
with friends, old or new.
And fun is good
for everyone!

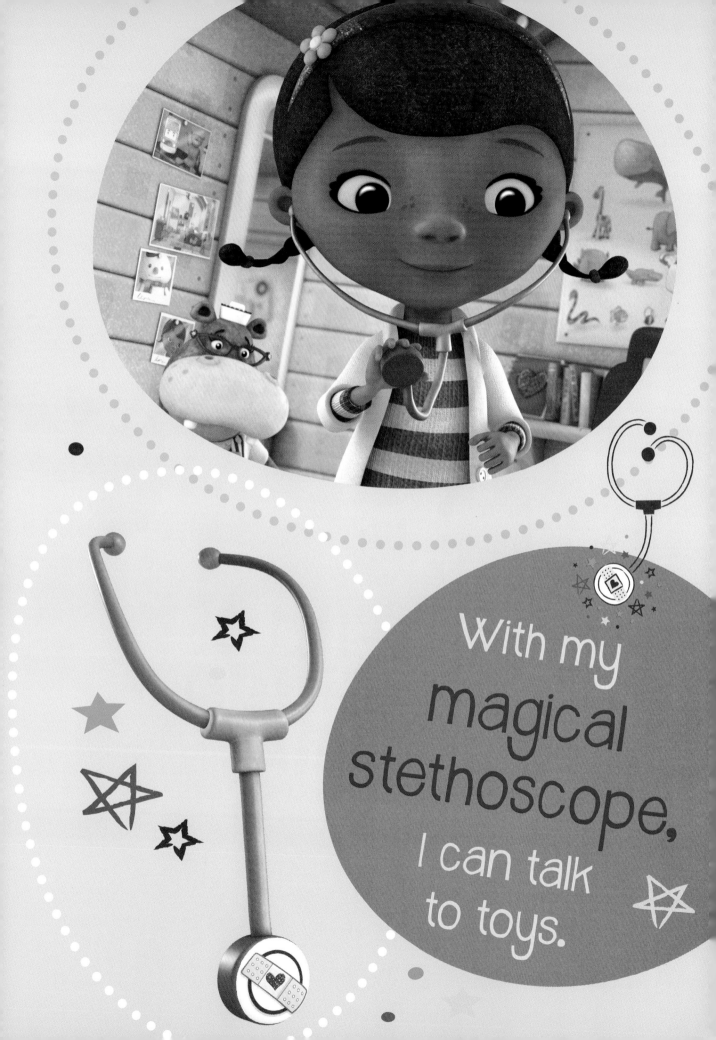

With my magical stethoscope, I can talk to toys.

Have you hugged a friend today?

CARING and SHARING make me feel GREAT.

FRIENDS

WELCOME

STUFF

FEELIN'

I'm
a big,
brave
dragon!

My friends make me jump for joy.

Caring ways make for happy days.

LAMBIE

This little lamb can cuddle

till the cows come home!

You can count on me.

I'VE GOT HUG-A-TUDE.

HALLIE

My friends keep me cool.

Professor Hootsburgh

Lam

nbie

STAND BY YOUR LAMB!

Together, we can solve any problem.

Won't you join us for tea?

Friends come in all shapes and sizes.

Some friends have wings!
Some friends have wheels!

Exercise your smile.

FRIENDS
STICK
TOGETHER.

Friends make me smile!

Come on, gang. Let's hold hands!

Hop on the caring wagon.

Will you be my friend?

CHECKUP TIME

Everyone gets
hurt sometimes.
Doc McStuffins is
there to make
the boo-boos
be gone.

DOC MCSTUFFINS' CLINIC

FOR TOYS AND STUFFED ANIMALS

THE DOC IS IN!

Friend on call!

I love making toys feel better.

A hippo always knows!

Let's check the Big Book of Boo-Boos.

It's time for your checkup.

STEP RIGHT UP.

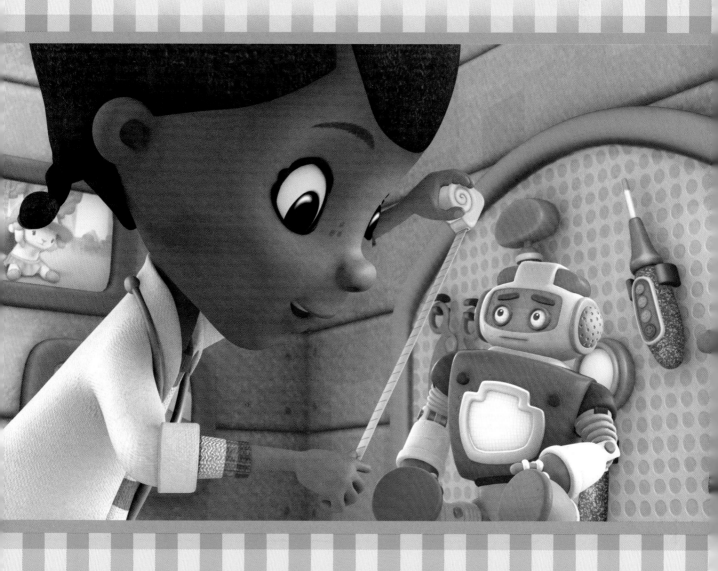

Let's do a few tests!

Let's
have
a look.

Let's have a listen.

It's okay.
Doc McStuffins
is on the case!

This will only tickle a little.

YOU'LL BE READY FOR
HUGGING AGAIN IN NO TIME!

I won't give up until I figure it out.

THIS WON'T HURT A BIT.

I have
a diagnosis!

LENNY NEEDS A LITTLE TLC:

Tender Loving Care

Someone has
Need-a-hugitis!

Susie Sunshine
has a case of
EYESWIDEITIS

Pricklethorns strike again!

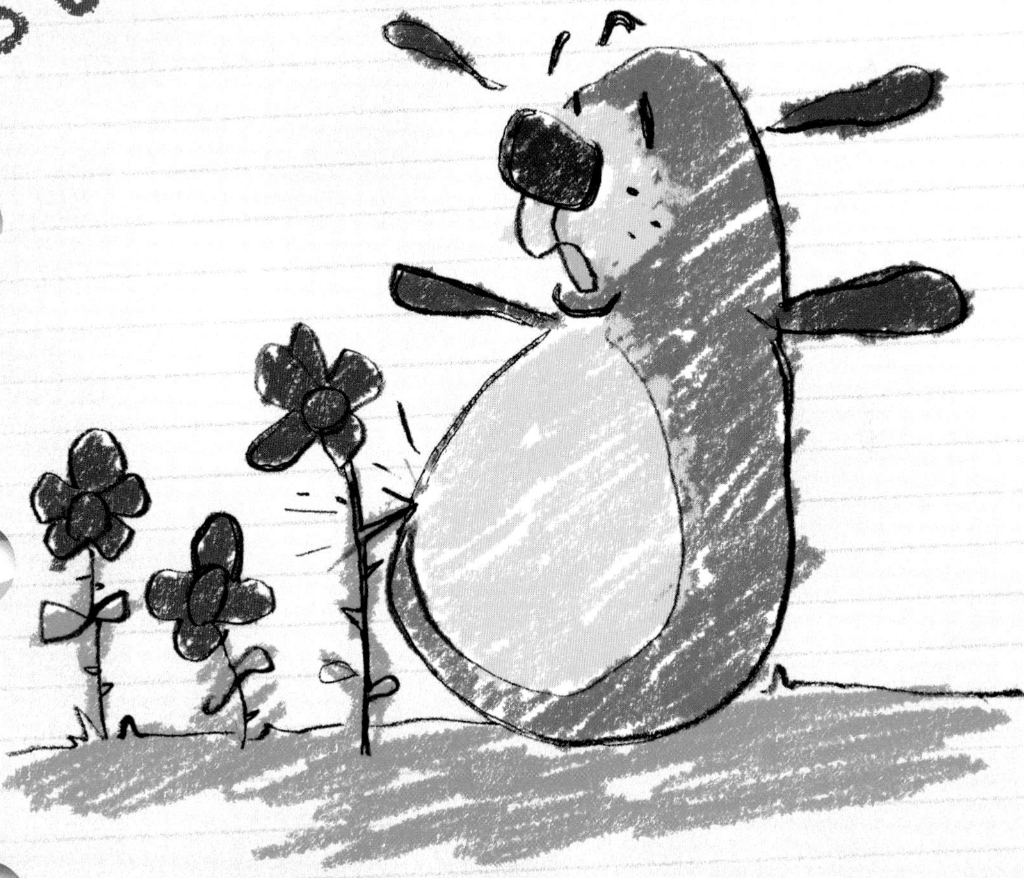

Looks like a case of Earstuffinosis

Bronto Boo-Boos!

After a rough case of
Splitheartitis,
Lambie needed some extra TLC.

FIRST, I AM GOING TO LISTEN TO YOUR HEART.

Your heart sounds great, Stuffy. It's a brave dragon heart.

Looks like a case of Bronto-breath. This is one for the Big Book of Boo-Boos!

You're in the hands of
the best toy doctor ever.

Hallie
is Doc's #1 helper!

It's Stuffy's turn to help.

DOC
TO THE RESCUE.

HERE TO HELP!

PLAYTIME

Doc, Lambie, Stuffy, and their friends are always ready for laughter and fun. They love going on adventures and trying new things.

Let's take
this party
outside!

Playing games is good for the heart.

HOW ABOUT A BRONTY-BACK RIDE?

HOP ON BOARD

Let's build a snowman!

Brrrr!

Doc and friends are on the move!

Prepare for blast off.

My prescription for you is to go outside and play!

Do you want to go stargazing?

stars, stars, planets, and stars,
I can see Jupiter.
I can see Mars!

Ready for laughter, ready for fun!

Ready for happy days spent in the sun!

I love
to play
games!

Zooooooooom!

Grab a hat!

It's dress-up time!

Marble mania with the gulpy, gulpy gators!

SURPRISE!

HAPPY BIRTHDAY, HALLIE!

Hearts and hugs

for everyone!

DOC'S ORDERS

Doc McStuffins has great ideas for staying happy and healthy— and having fun!

Don't forget to stretch.

Sometimes a nap is the perfect answer!

The more you rest, the better you feel.

Sunshine and exercise can help you glow.

Drink plenty of water to avoid Dried-out-a-tosis.

HEALTHY SNACKS ARE MADE FOR SHARING.

There's always **more** to learn and know.

Reading
feeds
your
imagination!

storytime is a special time.

Work together

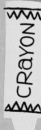

Four heads are better than one!

Hugs and happiness go hand in hand.

Healthy eyes sparkle!

D
O C
C U D
D L E S

Have cuddles, will share.

How about you?